Percy Bysshe Shelley

Rosalind and Helen, a Modern Eclogue

With other Poems

Percy Bysshe Shelley

Rosalind and Helen, a Modern Eclogue
With other Poems

ISBN/EAN: 9783337158057

Printed in Europe, USA, Canada, Australia, Japan

Cover: Foto ©Andreas Hilbeck / pixelio.de

More available books at **www.hansebooks.com**

ROSALIND AND HELEN

A MODERN ECLOGUE

With other Poems

BY

PERCY BYSSHE SHELLEY

A TYPE FAC-SIMILE OF THE

ORIGINAL EDITION OF MDCCCXIX

EDITED BY

H. BUXTON FORMAN

LONDON

PUBLISHED FOR THE SHELLEY SOCIETY

BY REEVES AND TURNER 196 STRAND

1888

ADVERTISEMENT.

The story of " Rosalind and Helen " is, undoubtedly, not an attempt in the highest style
of poetry. It is in no degree calculated to
excite profound meditation; and if, by interesting the affections and amusing the imagination, it awakens a certain ideal melancholy
favourable to the reception of more important
impressions, it will produce in the reader all
that the writer experienced in the composition.
I resigned myself, as I wrote, to the impulse of
the feelings which moulded the conception of
the story; and this impulse determined the
pauses of a measure, which only pretends to be
regular inasmuch as it corresponds with, and
expresses, the irregularity of the imaginations
which inspired it.

I do not know which of the few scattered
poems I left in England will be selected by

my bookseller, to add to this collection. One, which I sent from Italy, was written after a day's excursion among those lovely mountains which surround what was once the retreat, and where is now the sepulchre, of Petrarch. If any one is inclined to condemn the insertion of the introductory lines, which image forth the sudden relief of a state of deep despondency by the radiant visions disclosed by the sudden burst of an Italian sunrise in autumn on the highest peak of those delightful mountains, I can only offer as my excuse, that they were not erased at the request of a dear friend, with whom added years of intercourse only add to my apprehension of its value, and who would have had more right than any one to complain, that she has not been able to extinguish in me the very power of delineating sadness.

Naples, Dec. 20, 1818.

CONTENTS.

INTRODUCTION

INTRODUCTION

A GENEROUS member of the Shelley Society, who chooses to be unnamed and unknown, offered some time ago to present to his fellow members a reprint of one of the poet's volumes if I would undertake to edit it. Various circumstances combined to direct the choice to the volume issued in 1819 containing *Rosalind and Helen*, the *Lines written among the Euganean Hills*, the *Hymn to Intellectual Beauty*, and the sonnet entitled *Ozymandias*. The preparation of the reprint naturally leads to a few reflexions on the poetical contents of the original volume, and more particularly on that eclogue which occupies sixty-eight of the ninety-two pages composing the book ; and, on studying afresh that poem of which Shelley himself spoke or wrote so slightingly, I found myself once more in that atmosphere of reform which surrounds and permeates so many other works of the poet. Moreover this necessary re-perusal of an old favourite revives a well-worn impression that *Rosalind and Helen*, though disjointed and inconsistent in execution, is quite unusually replete with passages in a high degree beautiful and characteristic.

Shelley knew only too well how imperfect was his own work,—how imperfect was all human work, when judged by the elevated standard which he set up for himself and future aspirants to the poetic priesthood to follow; and his almost contemptuous attitude towards this particular child of his swift and splendid imagination is not difficult to understand. Yet I cannot bring myself to admit *Rosalind and Helen* to quite so low a place as he would seem to have assigned to it. Before attempting to examine the poem and the circumstances of its composition, let us look at what its author said about it. In the "Advertisement" prefixed to his own edition he frankly damns it with the faintest praise.

"The story of 'Rosalind and Helen' is," he says, "undoubtedly, not an attempt in the highest style of poetry. It is in no degree calculated to excite profound meditation; and if, by interesting the affections and amusing the imagination, it awaken a certain ideal melancholy favourable to the reception of more important impressions, it will produce in the reader all that the writer experienced in the composition. I resigned myself, as I wrote, to the impulse of the feelings which moulded the conception of the story; and this impulse determined the pauses of a measure, which only pretends to be regular inasmuch as it corresponds with, and expresses, the irregularity of the imaginations which inspired it."

By Mrs. Shelley we are told that *Rosalind and Helen* was begun at Marlow and thrown aside until she found it in Italy, when Shelley, at her request, finished it at the Baths of Lucca in the summer of 1818. When he had finished it, and Mrs. Shelley had transcribed it for the press, he wrote to Peacock of it that its structure was "slight and aëry, its subject ideal,"—adding in a later letter, "I lay no stress on it one way or the other. The concluding lines are natural."

Now the essential statement in all this is that the creation of *Rosalind and Helen* did no more than awaken in Shelley "a certain ideal melancholy favourable to the reception of more important impressions." To my apprehension it seems that the poem is properly to be regarded as a solid result of moral speculation rather than an exercise,—the outcome of impressions decidedly more important than any which can fairly be described by the term "ideal melancholy"; and what Shelley either forgets or modestly ignores is that those more important themes are there in the poem in such a form as to take effect at once on that receptiveness of the reader which he regards as the only probable result of his poem.

Let us look first at the story : who are Rosalind and Helen, and what have their lives produced for them at the time of their conversation forming the staple fabric of the poem ?

Rosalind and Helen are two young mothers at the time of their introduction to us, seemingly both of English middle-class birth, though of Helen's parents nothing is said. Rosalind, living with her mother, in her father's absence from England, has formed an attachment for a young man, who is about to marry her. When the pair are already at the altar her father suddenly appears from abroad, and forbids the banns on the ground that the bridegroom is his son by another mother than Rosalind's. The youth falls dead, but Rosalind lives on in self-contained misery. Her father dies leaving his wife and daughter unprovided for ; and Rosalind in sheer despair, and for her mother's sake, marries a man whom she positively loathes in the sequel, if not from the first. She has three children, all of whom fear their father like the plague. He in turn dies, leaving a will under which his widow is abominably traduced, and his children only provided for on condition of absolute separation from their mother. Rosalind accepts the position of a childless outcast rather than expose her offspring to the horrors of poverty.

With a good deal of the fierce resolve of a martyr, Rosalind from first to last has been the slave of conventional duty. Not so Helen, who loves, from Rosalind's point of view " not wisely but too well," Lionel, a youth of noble birth, amiable character, great personal attractions, and revolutionary-humanitarian sentiments and convictions. Rosalind, apparently at a time anterior to her own dire misfortunes, considers Helen's relations with Lionel sufficient cause for breaking with her friend. Lionel throws himself as orator and pamphleteer into the ferment of agitation against political, social, and priestly tyranny ; and, when the popular hope dies for the moment, and tyranny and superstition are triumphantly consolidated in power, the frustrated spirit of freedom within him drives him forth to wander in far lands, away from Helen, and not unsuspected of seeking solace in strange loves. After three years he returns,

C

desolate, and renews his intercourse with Helen, under whose influence his spirit has a second birth of faith, hope, and power to agitate, while his bodily health begins to fail. Although Helen's account is a trifle vague, there seems to me to be no doubt that, during this spiritual revival, Lionel was conducting a second courtship of Helen, the end of which is that she consents to a second union with him of the same unconventional character as the first. No sooner is this matter settled than Lionel is arrested on a charge of uttering a blasphemous and seditious libel of and concerning Almighty God and of and concerning the Holy Scriptures,—to translate into the jargon of the contemporary law-courts the flowing poetic generalities of Helen's narrative. " Soon, but too late," Lionel is released from prison, and proceeds in a carriage from London to his home in the Welsh mountains near the coast, with the stamp of death already on him ; and there, after a short time, he dies. Helen goes mad, is tended by Lionel's mother, and gives birth to a son. When she recovers her reason she learns for the first time that she is a mother, that Lionel's mother has died during her period of insanity, that Lionel has left great wealth to her by will, and that "the ready lies of law" have bereft her and her child of all. She commences an action to vindicate her legal rights ; but what came of it is not recorded. Whatever the result of her lawsuit, Helen acquires a home with her little son on the banks of the Lake of Como, where Rosalind takes up her abode with her early friend. Eventually Rosalind's daughter is restored to her (we hear no more of her other two children), and grows up with Helen's son ; and the young people are at last married, or rather, I should say, consecrated to each other, for we are not told whether in this respect they followed the orthodox traditions of Rosalind or the anti-matrimonial heresy of Lionel and Helen. Of the two friends Rosalind dies prematurely, while Helen lives to be old and dies among her relations.

Such in brief is the argument of *Rosalind and Helen:* I have interpreted the details of the narrative literally and set them down in commonplace terms, in order to emphasize and bring home to the mind the fundamental

conceptions which Shelley has embodied in so much
poetry and overlaid with so much of his characteristic
propagandism, that the mind is apt to dwell upon
isolated passages rather than lay hold on the fable as
a whole. No doubt the poet had good reasons for leading the attention of Peacock to the ideal side of the
subject; but probably Peacock's wit was far too keenly
edged for the real basis of the work to escape him,
although he may perhaps not have discovered what
Shelley may perhaps have been most anxious to have
undiscovered, namely, that the relations of Rosalind and
Helen were a reproduction of the relations of Mary
Wollstonecraft Shelley and an early friend,—a reproduction highly idealized, be it conceded, but still a reproduction.

Whatever Peacock may have known or divined on
this subject, he can scarcely have failed to recognize his
friend's delightful self-portraiture in Lionel; for this is
one of the thinnest of the disguises in which Shelley
has masked the essential characteristics of his personality,—that personality which Peacock had himself been
caricaturing as Scythrop, in my opinion rather wildly
and remotely, in his charming book *Nightmare Abbey*,
published in 1818. Nor is it likely that the author
of *Nightmare Abbey*, when he read for Shelley the proof-
sheets of *Rosalind and Helen* and recognized in Lionel
the lineaments of which he had just given the world so
different a representation in Scythrop, failed to observe
in what particular popular agitation it was that Lionel
figured as taking part. For, although the terms are
large enough to be applicable to the French Revolution,
the local colour is wholly English; and I cannot avoid
the conclusion that here we have nothing more or less
than an idealized record of the Reform agitation of
1816 and 1817. That very collapse of the democratic
aspirations which Shelley witnessed in 1817 finds its
appropriate place in *Rosalind and Helen*; and the final
outrage of Lionel's imprisonment on a charge of blasphemy is precisely what Shelley was in constant risk
of experiencing himself, and had been ever since his
boyhood.

I have already referred to the basis of that part of

the poem which deals especially with the relations between the two women whose names it bears ; and I
cannot better enlarge on this point than by quoting a
passage from the second volume of Professor Dowden's
Life of Shelley, in which we read at pages 130 and 131
as follows :—

" It can hardly be doubted that the incidents and feelings
portrayed were to some extent suggested to Shelley by Mary's
relations with the friend of her girlhood, in the old Dundee days—
Isabel Baxter. Since Mary's flight from her father's house in
July, 1814, Isabel had fallen away from friendship. Now she
herself a wife, and rumours, probably false rumours, reached Mary
that Isabel was not a happy wife. A visit of Isabel's father,
William Baxter, to Marlow, in September, tended to draw the
alienated friends once more together ; and when it was proposed
that Isabel Booth should be Mary's companion on the journey to
Italy, she would gladly have acceded to the proposal. But David
Booth, her husband, no ordinary man, had heard scandalous and
lying tales of Shelley's life ; his strong moral sense was shocked by
the thought of danger to his wife's character or fame, and sternly
yet tenderly he forbade a renewal of the intimacy. So by the Lake
of Como there was no meeting, like that represented in the poem,
of the sundered friends."

Now although we must not for a moment mix up in
our minds the stalwart-minded David Booth and the
inconceivably despicable wretch whom Shelley has in-
vented for a mate to Rosalind,—although, indeed, we
may accept both Rosalind and her husband as ideal per-
sonalities created for the purpose of giving expression
to Shelley's views on certain matters of personal con-
duct, still I think it probable that this episode in Mary's
history not only "to some extent suggested" certain
incidents, but was the predominating influence which
drove Shelley to set about his eclogue. If so, the record
just quoted is doubly interesting as establishing approxi-
mately the time of Shelley's first occupation with
Rosalind and Helen. That the poem was begun at
Marlow we know from Mrs. Shelley, but not whether
early or late in 1817, or whether during the summer
which was mainly devoted to *Laon and Cythna*. It was
in September, as we learn from Professor Dowden, that
Laon and Cythna was finished—the 23rd of September ;

and by the 26th Mrs. Shelley was already bewailing the
enforced abandonment of the eclogue; so that, if the
Baxter incidents of that month were the beginning of the
scheme, he must have been working on both poems at
once; for he left Marlow for London on the day of *Laon
and Cythna's* completion; and, while in London, he
seems to have communicated to Mary an injunction of
Abernethy's pupil, William Lawrence, " to cease from
the exciting toil of composition, and to seek the benefits
of rest and change of air." [1] On hearing this, Mary wrote
to him, " It is well that your poem [meaning *Laon and
Cythna*] was finished before this edict was issued against
the imagination; but my pretty eclogue will suffer from
it." [2] Whether the composition was resumed at Marlow
in defiance of the edict, I do not know; but if not,
Shelley had already done enough of it to commit to the
press; for, before finally quitting England on the 12th
of March 1818, he had confided the poem, or a part
of it, to his publisher, Mr. Ollier. This was probably
the portion copied by Mary at Marlow as recorded in her
diary under date the 19th of February 1818; and the
original manuscript most likely went to Italy with them.
Perhaps, when the poem was completed in August 1818
at the Baths of Lucca, and Shelley wrote to Peacock as
if Mary had just then copied it all out, he had so far
altered the original scheme as to make a fresh copy
of the whole necessary.

I have not failed to deprecate the confusion of David
Booth with Rosalind's husband as depicted by Shelley;
but we must now look a little more closely at the Baxter-
Booth circle, as we find it delineated in Professor Dowden's *Life of Shelley*. In the house of William Baxter
at Dundee, Mary had, it seems, " spent some of the
happiest months of her girlhood," finding " close and
dear companions " in his daughters, Christy and Isabel;
but, although Baxter was a man of such liberal views
as to merit and incur expulsion from the sect of Glass-
ites which his forefathers had helped to establish at
Dundee, and although, to boot, he was Godwin's ardent

[1] Dowden's *Life of Shelley*, vol. ii., p. 129.
[2] *Ibid.*

admirer as well as his friend, Isabel's friendship was
withdrawn on Mary's flight with Shelley in 1814. David
Booth, to whom Isabel was led to ally herself in a union
far more strange though more orthodox, was many
years older than her father, "a self-educated man of
vigorous intellect, imperious will, and disposition impe-
riously kind, . . . not five feet high, very dark of hue,
with eyes red and watery, and something of the imp, if
not the fiend, in his look." It seems he was a brewer
and afterwards a schoolmaster, recognized in and about
Newburgh as "a person of stupendous learning and
mysterious power." He "was in principles a republican,"
and it was "whispered that he had sold himself to the
devil for learning."

If it was also whispered, as we have seen, that
the young girl who had surrendered her life into the
keeping of this elderly curiosity was not a happy wife,
the whisperers had certainly some show of reason on
their side : at all events, when Baxter had found out
how unaltered Mary was by her union with Shelley,
which by the bye was now duly conventionalized, and
how entirely amiable, frugal in personal habits, benevo-
lent, and delicately considerate of others, was the man
of genius to whom she had given herself,—when the
sometime Glassite of Dundee had told all this to his
daughter, her devotion to her brewer was not so enthrall-
ing but that she would gladly have "made it up" with
Mary and accompanied the Shelleys to Italy. But
David Booth said "No." In November 1817, both
Booth and Baxter spent an evening with the Shelleys in
London ; and before the close of the year the sturdy
little brewer, whether seeing in the attractions of that
charming society an element of danger to his wife's peace
and his own, or finding Shelley's views in morals and
politics really too wide for even his republican swallow,
over-ruled the tolerant impulsiveness of his too facile,
not to say frisky, young father-in-law (Baxter was a little
over forty), and decreed eternal separation. The verdict
was communicated to Shelley by Baxter; and the poet
took the close of the episode in such a serious, frank,
and dignified spirit that I cannot resist the temptation
to reproduce here his letter to Baxter on the subject,

more especially as it contains some useful backward glimpses. This is the letter :[1]—

"Marlow, December 30, 1817.

" MY DEAR SIR,

"Your candid explanation is very welcome to me, as it relieves me from a weight of uncertainty, and is consistent with my own mode of treating those who honour me with their friendship— which is, either to maintain with them a free and unsuspicious intercourse, or explicitly to state to them my motives for interrupting or circumscribing it, so soon as they arise within my own mind.

" I understand by your letter that you decline, in the name of your family, an intercourse which I believe had its sole foundation in the intimacy of Isabel and Mary. This intercourse entirely originated in an unsolicited advance on their part ;[2] a change in their opinions and feelings produced it then, and now concludes it. Mary renewed with pleasure the friendship of her early years. I considered her friends as mine, and found much satisfaction, distinct from that duty, in discovering in you, the first of the new circle to whom I was introduced, a man of virtue and talent with whose feelings and opinions I perpetually found occasions of sympathy. To me, a secluded valetudinarian, all this was quite an event. Mary for three whole years had been lamenting the loss of her friend, and was made miserable and indignant that her friendship had been sacrificed to opinions which she supposed had already received their condemnation in the mind of every enlightened reasoner on moral science. Young and ardent spirits confound theory and practice. *I* saw that all this was in the natural order of things, and it is neither my habit to feel indignation or disappointment at the inconsistencies of mankind. People who had one atom of pride or resentment for injury or neglect would have refused the renewal of an intimacy which had already been once dissolved on a plea, in their conception, to the last degree unworthy and erroneous. I thus see your determination to deprive Mary of the intercourse of her friend, and most highly respect the motives, as I know they must exist in your mind, for this proceeding. May I ask *precisely what* those motives are ? You do not distinctly say, but only allude to certain free opinions which I hold, inconsistent with yours. We had a good deal of discussion about all sorts of opinions, and I thought we agreed on all—except matters of taste ; and I don't think any serious consequences ought to flow from a controversy whether Wordsworth or Campbell be the greater poet. Yet I would not be misapprehended. Though I have not a spark of pride or resentment in this matter, I disdain to say a word that should tend to *persuade*

---

[1] Dowden's *Life of Shelley*, vol. ii., pp. 175-8.

[2] " Consequent," says Professor Dowden, " on Godwin's informing Mr. Baxter in May of the fact of Shelley's marriage, celebrated in December, 1816."

you to change your decision. On any such change you know where to find a man constant and sincere in his predilections. But all I now want is to know the plain truth.

" Mr. Booth is no doubt a man of great intellectual acuteness and consummate skill in the exercise of logic. I never met with a man by whom, in the short time we exchanged ideas, I felt myself excited to so much severe and sustained mental competition, or from whom I derived so much amusement and instruction. It would have given me much pleasure to have cultivated his acquaintance. But I know that this desire could not be reciprocal. Nor is it difficult to apprehend the cause of this distinction. Am I not right in my conjecture in attributing to Mr. Booth the change in your sentiment announced in your letter? His keen and subtle mind, deficient in those elementary feelings which are the *principles* of all moral reasoning, is better fitted for the detection of error than the establishment of truth, and his pleadings, urged or withdrawn with sceptical caution and indifference, may be employed with almost equal force as an instrument of fair argument or sophistry. In matters of abstract speculation we can readily recur to the first principles on which our opinions rest, and thus confute a sophism or derive instruction from an argument. But in the complicated relations of private life, it is a practice difficult, dangerous, and rare to appeal to an elementary principle ; the motives of the sophist are many and secret ; the resources of his ingenuity as numerous as the relations respecting which it is exercised. Mr. Booth's reasonings *may* be right ; they *may* be sincere ; he *may* be conscientiously impressed with views widely differing from mine. But be frank with me, my dear sir ; is it not Mr. Booth who has persuaded you to see things in this way since your last visit, when no such considerations as you allege in your letter were present to your thoughts? The only motive that suggests this question is an unwillingness to submit to the having my intimacies made the sport of secret and unacknowledged manœuvres.

" I need not say that your expressions of kindness and service are flattering to me, and that I can say with great truth that I should consider myself honoured if at any time it were possible that you would make the limited power which I possess a source of utility to you.

" My dear Sir,
" Yours most sincerely,
" P. B. SHELLEY."

To this delightful letter Mary added the following pretty postscript :—

" MY DEAR SIR,
" You see I prophesied well three months ago, when you were here. I then said that I was sure that Mr. Booth was averse to our intercourse, and would find some means to break it off. I

wish I had you by the fire here in my little study, and it might be 'double, double, toil and trouble,' but I could quickly convince you that your girls are not below me in station, and that in fact I am the fittest companion for them in the world ; but I postpone the argument until I see you, for I know (pardon me) that *viva voce* is all in all with you."

Baxter, it seems, showed the letter to Booth, who wrote thus to Shelley :[1]—

"You have amused yourself in sketching the characters of Mr. Baxter and me. They are composition pictures, and as a pair of portraits form together a ludicrous, mystical Duality, combining the abstract principles of good and of evil—of Divinity and of Demon."

It is regret-worthy that we have not the whole composition before us; but it seems to have ended thus :—

"I have only to add that Mr. Baxter's (to which yours now before me is an answer) was written and sent off without having been shown to me. I certainly should not have suggested any expressions which could have called forth remarks about rank or station. In these I never would acknowledge inferiority, and at all events they have nothing to do with the present question."

Shelley saw Baxter again on the 2nd of March, when preparing for his journey to the Continent ; but, although Isabel Booth was in London at the time, no communication took place between her and Mary. It appears that the latest expressions from the Shelleys to the Baxters were of the sincerest good-will and solicitude.

We all know that, although Shelley, urged by motives more or less unselfish, was three times married, twice to Harriett and once to Mary, he was an ardent disbeliever in the institution of marriage, in which he saw an instrument of tyranny and oppression. We all know how eagerly he desired to see reform in the marriage laws and in the views of society concerning the relations of the sexes. We have seen in his letter to Baxter—who, by the bye, told Mary,[2] he thought the anti-matrimonial *Queen Mab* "the best poem of modern days"—that Mary had lamented for three years the rupture of her friendship with Isabel and had been made miserable and indignant by the sacrifice of that friendship to a matter

[1] Dowden's *Life of Shelley*, vol. ii., p. 178.
[2] *Ibid.* p. 144.

of opinion practically concerning the institution of
marriage. In David Booth, Shelley evidently saw a
man prone to tyrannize over those with whom he came
in contact, and it is clear that he respected the little
brewer's intellect more than his heart. And yet he saw
this young girl indissolubly bound to David Booth—
destined to pass her life in the society and under the
tutelage of a man, to say the least, unengaging—a man
under whose dictatorship she and her family were de-
prived of all communication with a dear friend of her
own sex and years. This to Shelley would naturally
seem intolerable tyranny ; and no wonder that he was
stirred to read the world a fresh homily on this text,
concerning marriage and free union. No wonder that
one of the heroines of his next poem should address
the other thus on meeting her beside the Lake of
Como :—

> " None doth behold us now : the power
> That led us forth at this lone hour
> Will be but ill requited
> If thou depart in scorn : oh ! come,
> And talk of our abandoned home.
> Remember, this is Italy,
> And we are exiles.   Talk with me
> Of that our land, whose wilds and floods,
> Barren and dark although they be,
> Were dearer than these chestnut woods :
> Those heathy paths, that inland stream,
> And the blue mountains, shapes which seem
> Like wrecks of childhood's sunny dream :
> Which that we have abandoned now,
> Weighs on the heart like that remorse
> Which altered friendship leaves.   I seek
> No more our youthful intercourse.
> That cannot be !   Rosalind, speak,
> Speak to me.   Leave me not.—When morn did come,
> When evening fell upon our common home,
> When for one hour we parted,—do not frown :
> I would not chide thee, though thy faith is broken :
> But turn to me.   Oh ! by this cherished token,
> Of woven hair, which thou wilt not disown,
> Turn, as 'twere but the memory of me,
> And not my scorned self who prayed to thee."

Nor is it strange that, in reading his homily on the
tyranny of wedlock, Shelley should so far have idealized

the conception of a tyrant husband as to endow him liberally with the meanest vices.

> " He was a man
> Hard, selfish, loving only gold,
> Yet full of guile : his pale eyes ran
> With tears, which each some falsehood told,
> And oft his smooth and bridled tongue
> Would give the lie to his flushing cheek :
> He was a coward to the strong :
> He was a tyrant to the weak,
> On whom his vengeance he would wreak :
> For scorn, whose arrows search the heart,
> From many a stranger's eye would dart,
> And on his memory cling, and follow
> His soul to its home so cold and hollow.
> *   *   *   *   *
> He died :
> I know not how : he was not old,
> If age be numbered by its years :
> But he was bowed and bent with fears,
> Pale with the quenchless thirst of gold,
> Which, like fierce fever, left him weak ;
> And his strait lip and bloated cheek
> Were warped in spasms by hollow sneers ;
> And selfish cares with barren plough,
> Not age, had lined his narrow brow,
> And foul and cruel thoughts, which feed
> Upon the withering life within,
> Like vipers on some poisonous weed.
> Whether his ill were death or sin
> None knew, until he died indeed,
> And then men owned they were the same."

Rosalind's separation from her children under her dead husband's will is, of course, the reflexion of Shelley's separation from his children through the action of their dead mother's relations ; and as, in the Chancery suit of these people, the argument had been used that Shelley's views of marriage led to immorality according to the legal standard of morals, it was a natural relief to the outraged father to emphasize in his fiction the moral evils of marriage without love : certainly he leads the reader's sympathies with great delicacy and dexterity to the side of Helen, who trusted herself and her happiness unreservedly to Lionel because she loved him, rather than of Rosalind, who sold herself body and soul to one whom she not only did not love but whom she absolutely contemned and loathed. Her price was food, lodging, and respectability for herself and her mother. Her mother soon died ; her husband, from his "putrid shroud" as Shelley says, lyingly denied her respectability ; and when his death had shaken her free from what she described as "those abhorred embraces," she underwent the frightful experience of reading / in her involuntary and irrepressible joy at his death, the condemnation of her own dutifully ordered life.

Rosalind's story is indeed far from a pleasant or even an interesting one ; and it is in Helen's that we find the agreeable side of the poem. Devoted to the memory of Lionel, she gives her friend an enthusiastic account of his genius and amiable qualities ; and that account is, as I have said, full of the personality of Shelley and his views upon reform. It tells of the time

> "When liberty's dear pæan fell
> 'Mid murderous howls. To Lionel,
> Though of great wealth and lineage high,
> Yet through those dungeon walls there came
> Thy thrilling light, O liberty !
> And as the meteor's midnight flame
> Startles the dreamer, sun-like truth
> Flashed on his visionary youth,
> And filled him, not with love, but faith,
> And hope, and courage . . . "

The restless and reckless propagandism of Lionel is clearly Shelley's own experience but slightly idealized, and the account of the wonder it inspired in commonplace minds might have been translated from the prose of some commentators on Shelley's doings as a reform agitator :

> " Men wondered, and some sneered to see
> One sow what he could never reap :
> For he is rich, they said, and young,
> And might drink from the depths of luxury.
> If he seeks fame, fame never crowned
> The champion of a trampled creed :
> If he seeks power, power is enthroned
> 'Mid antient rights and wrongs, to feed
> Which hungry wolves with praise and spoil,
> Those who would sit near power must toil ;
> And such, there sitting, all may see.
> What seeks he ? All that others seek

> He casts away, like a vile weed
> Which the sea casts unreturningly.
> That poor and hungry men should break
> The laws which wreak them toil and scorn
> We understand ; but Lionel
> We know is rich and nobly born."

Then the account of the "wild and queer" verses about "devils and saints and all such gear," which he aimed against the priests and so incurred their hatred, is very suggestive of foundation in fact; and, if the following passage had occurred in a poem headed "England in 1817-18," who would have wondered ?—

> "Grey Power was seated
> Safely on her ancestral throne ;
> And Faith, the Python, undefeated,
> Even to its blood-stained steps dragged on
> Her foul and wounded train, and men
> Were trampled and deceived again,
> And words and shews again could bind
> The wailing tribes of human kind
> In scorn and famine."

If we had met the next few lines in prose in Mary's journal for 1814, we should scarcely have been surprised :—

> "Then he would bid me not to weep,
> And say with flattery false, yet sweet,
> That death and he could never meet,
> If I would never part with him.
> And so we loved, and did unite
> All that in us was yet divided :
> For when he said, that many a rite,
> By men to bind but once provided,
> Could not be shared by him and me,
> Or they would kill him in their glee,
> I shuddered, and then laughing said—
> ' We will have rites our faith to bind,
> But our church shall be the starry night,
> Our altar the grassy earth outspread,
> And our priest the muttering wind.' "

And a page or two further on we emerge with certainty into the region of the actual in a curious way enough ; for when Lionel has been taken for sedition and blasphemy, as Shelley was quite prepared to be, he

F

cries to Helen as she is driven forth from the prison she
would fain share with him:

> " Fear not the tyrants shall rule for ever,
> Or the priests of the bloody faith ;
> They stand on the brink of that mighty river,
> Whose waves they have tainted with death :
> It is fed from the depths of a thousand dells,
> Around them it foams, and rages, and swells,
> And their swords and their sceptres I floating see,
> Like wrecks in the surge of eternity."

This stanza is really one of six addressed by Shelley
to his infant son William, between the time of the Lord
Chancellor's decree depriving him of the custody of
Harriett's children and the time of the final departure
for Italy—I should say in March 1818 ; for there are
allusions to the sea and the boat in other stanzas which
make it probable the poem was composed on the rough
passage in the boat *Lady Castlereagh* that carried Shelley
and his family from Dover to Calais, and written down
perhaps at the end of that stormy voyage. When Mrs.
Shelley printed the verses to William in 1839, she gave
the second line with the epithet *evil* instead of *bloody*—
a change which leaves the verse, if more polite, still less
forcible and characteristic ; but the words are for the
rest practically identical. It would be interesting to
know whether, when Shelley addressed his son on the
subject of their flight from England, he repeated the eight
lines from a part of his eclogue already completed, or
whether, when he revised the eclogue in Italy, he was
tempted to insert in it this very appropriate stanza of
his little poem. I lean to the latter supposition ; but
know of no external evidence on the subject.

It is not necessary to elaborate the evidence of what
few will be disposed to dispute, to wit, the position that
the motives of this poem of *Rosalind and Helen* are before
all things personal and homiletic ; nor need I enter on
a long analysis of the faults of execution which show
how feeble a hold the story, as a story, had on Shelley's
imagination. The principal flaws are inconsistencies in
the narrative of Rosalind, which is precisely where we
should expect the interest of Shelley in his own creation

to relax, seeing that her character was just such as he would be most likely to contemn.   Hence it is no great marvel that Rosalind, the mother of three children, who at one point speaks of her two wild boys as cowering fearfully near her knee while the babe at her bosom was hushed with fear at its father's approach, thus making the girl the youngest, should so far forget herself in the sequel as to mention her daughter as the first-born. Similarly we do not think much of her inconsistency when, after promising Helen to tell her the truth, she first says she watched her husband's unlamented tomb morning and evening, and would not depart from it, while her children " laughed aloud in frantic glee," and afterwards affirms that she went away from the place immediately after the reading of the will without even noticing her children. But if Rosalind and her story had had for Shelley an interest other than didactic these things would probably have been obvious to him.

These flaws, such as they are, are left upon the poem for all time, for it was Shelley's will not to bring his work to perfection.   To the few errors in the sense which Peacock's unsympathetic revision of the proofs failed to detect, and which gave Shelley some small concern, we may yet hope to see justice done in time ; for it would be strange if the original manuscript and Mrs. Shelley's copy had both disappeared for ever: meanwhile rather than bewail our ignorance as to the particular passages which were thus corrupted, let us congratulate ourselves that the noble close of the poem is free from corruption, and that most of the many flashes of self-revelation which Shelley vouchsafed us in the portraiture of Lionel are unimpaired by their passage through the press.[1]

---

[1] The bare text here reprinted requires for pleasurable reading the following corrections and suggestions :—

Page 6 line 11.   For *thee* read *there.*

Page 18, line 9.   Omit the turned commas.

Pages 23-4.   This passage is probably corrupt.   It is possible that *Which* in the last line but one of page 23 is a misprint for *While,* and *and* in line 2 of page 24 a misprint for *had.*

Page 33, line 2.   The words *nursling child* may be right, but are suspicious.   They form something very like a pleonasm ; whereas *nursing child* is a familiar equivalent for *a child at nurse.*

Page 40, line 8.   For *striken* read *stricken.*

It has often pleased me to connect in my mind with the name of Shelley that memorable stanza of the Poet Laureate's—

> "The poet in a golden clime was born,
>   With golden stars above ;
> Dower'd with the hate of hate, the scorn of scorn,
>   The love of love."

Indeed, apart from the golden clime, I know of no one to whom that stanza applies so perfectly ; and of all the fictitious characters in Shelley's poetry that serve to bring his own personality before us in various phases and modifications,—Laon, Athanase, the poet in *Alastor*, Lionel,—I think the one that renders most of the essential spirit of Shelley is Lionel. It would not be far from the truth if we applied to Shelley the words of Helen concerning Lionel—

> "love and life in him were twins,
> Born at one birth : in every other
> First life then love its course begins,
> Though they be children of one mother ;
> And so through this dark world they fleet
> Divided, till in death they meet :
> But he loved all things ever."

H. BUXTON FORMAN.

46 MARLBOROUGH HILL, ST. JOHN'S WOOD,
      October 1888.

Page 60, lines 11-14. Whether lax, licentious, or eccentric in its construction or diction, I do not doubt this passage is what Shelley wrote.

Page 61, lines 9-11. To bring out the sense of these lines the punctuation should be that adopted by Mr. Rossetti :—

> "O that I were now dead ! but such
> (Did they not, love, demand too much,
> Those dying murmurs ?) he forbade."

"But such he forbade" means, of course, "but he forbade me to put myself to death."

Page 62, line 12. For *rescued* read *rescue.*

Page 63, line 12. The final comma is probably a misprint.

Page 77, line 9. The word *songs* seems to me suspiciously like a misprint for *sons.*

Page 89, lines 5 and 6 from foot. For *lover's* read *lovers'* ; and for *are* read *art.*

Page 91, line 1. For *loves* read *love's.*

ROSALIND AND HELEN,

A

MODERN ECLOGUE.

ROSALIND AND HELEN.

Rosalind, Helen and her Child.

Scene, the Shore of the Lake of Como.

HELEN.

COME hither, my sweet Rosalind.
'Tis long since thou and I have met;
And yet methinks it were unkind
Those moments to forget.
Come sit by me.   I see thee stand
By this lone lake, in this far land,
Thy loose hair in the light wind flying,
Thy sweet voice to each tone of even
United, and thine eyes replying
To the hues of yon fair heaven.
Come, gentle friend: wilt sit by me?
And be as thou wert wont to be

Ere we were disunited?
None doth behold us now: the power
That led us forth at this lone hour
Will be but ill requited
If thou depart in scorn: oh! come,
And talk of our abandoned home.
Remember, this is Italy,
And we are exiles.   Talk with me
Of that our land, whose wilds and floods,
Barren and dark although they be,
Were dearer than these chesnut woods:
Those heathy paths, that inland stream,
And the blue mountains, shapes which seem
Like wrecks of childhood's sunny dream:
Which that we have abandoned now,
Weighs on the heart like that remorse
Which altered friendship leaves.   I seek
No more our youthful intercourse.
That cannot be! Rosalind, speak,
Speak to me.   Leave me not.—When morn
          did come,
When evening fell upon our common home,

When for one hour we parted,—do not frown:
I would not chide thee, though thy faith is
          broken:
But turn to me.   Oh! by this cherished token,
Of woven hair, which thou wilt not disown,
Turn, as 'twere but the memory of me,
And not my scorned self who prayed to thee.

ROSALIND.

Is it a dream, or do I see
And hear frail Helen ?   I would flee
Thy tainting touch; but former years
Arise, and bring forbidden tears;
And my o'erburthened memory
Seeks yet its lost repose in thee.
I share thy crime.   I cannot choose
But weep for thee : mine own strange grief
But seldom stoops to such relief:
Nor ever did I love thee less,
Though mourning o'er thy wickedness
Even with a sister's woe.   I knew
What to the evil world is due,

And therefore sternly did refuse
To link me with the infamy
Of one so lost as Helen.   Now
Bewildered by my dire despair,
Wondering I blush, and weep that thou
Should'st love me still,—thou only ! —There,
Let us sit on that grey stone,
Till our mournful talk be done.

HELEN.

Alas ! not there ; I cannot bear
The murmur of this lake to hear.
A sound from thee, Rosalind dear,
Which never yet I heard elsewhere
But in our native land, recurs,   ·
Even here where now we meet.   It stirs
Too much of suffocating sorrow !
In the dell of yon dark chesnut wood
Is a stone seat, a solitude   ·
Less like our own.   The ghost of peace
Will not desert this spot.   To-morrow,

If thy kind feelings should not cease,
We may sit here.

ROSALIND.

Thou lead, my sweet,
And I will follow.

HENRY.

'Tis Fenici's seat
Where you are going ? This is not the way,
Mamma; it leads behind those trees that grow
Close to the little river.

HELEN.

Yes : I know :
I was bewildered. Kiss me, and be gay,
Dear boy : why do you sob ?

HENRY.

I do not know :
But it might break any one's heart to see
You and the lady cry so bitterly.

HELEN.

It is a gentle child, my friend. Go home,
Henry, and play with Lilla till I come.
We only cried with joy to see each other ;
We are quite merry now : Good night.

                    The boy
Lifted a sudden look upon his mother,
And in the gleam of forced and hollow joy
Which lightened o'er her face, laughed with
          the glee
Of light and unsuspecting infancy,
And whispered in her ear, " Bring home with
          you
That sweet strange lady-friend."   Then off he
          flew,
But stopt, and beckoned with a meaning smile,
Where the road turned. Pale Rosalind the while,
Hiding her face, stood weeping silently.

In silence then they took the way
Beneath the forest's solitude.

It was a vast and antique wood,
Thro' which they took their way ;
And the grey shades of evening
O'er that green wilderness did fling
Still deeper solitude.
Pursuing still the path that wound
The vast and knotted trees around
Thro' which slow shades were wandering,
To a deep lawny dell they came,
To a stone seat beside a spring,
O'er which the columned wood did frame
A roofless temple, like the fane
Where, ere new creeds could faith obtain,
Man's early race once knelt beneath
The overhanging deity.
O'er this fair fountain hung the sky,
Now spangled with rare stars. The snake,
The pale snake, that with eager breath
Creeps here his noontide thirst to slake,
Is beaming with many a mingled hue,
Shed from yon dome's eternal blue,
When he floats on that dark and lucid flood

In the light of his own loveliness;
And the birds that in the fountain dip
Their plumes, with fearless fellowship
Above and round him wheel and hover.
The fitful wind is heard to stir
One solitary leaf on high ;
The chirping of the grasshopper
Fills every pause.   There is emotion
In all that dwells at noontide here :
Then, thro' the intricate wild wood,
A maze of life and light and motion
Is woven.   But there is stillness now :
Gloom, and the trance of Nature now :
The snake is in his cave asleep ;
The birds are on the branches dreaming :
Only the shadows creep :
Only the glow-worm is gleaming :
Only the owls and the nightingales
Wake in this dell when day-light fails,
And grey shades gather in the woods :
And the owls have all fled far away
In a merrier glen to hoot and play,

For the moon is veiled and sleeping now.
The accustomed nightingale still broods
On her accustomed bough,
But she is mute ; for her false mate
Has fled and left her desolate.

This silent spot tradition old
Had peopled with the spectral dead.
For the roots of the speaker's hair felt cold
And stiff, as with tremulous lips he told
That a hellish shape at midnight led
The ghost of a youth with hoary hair,
And sate on the seat beside him there,
Till a naked child came wandering by,
When the fiend would change to a lady fair !
A fearful tale ! The truth was worse :
For here a sister and a brother
Had solemnized a monstrous curse,
Meeting in this fair solitude :
For beneath yon very sky,
Had they resigned to one another
Body and soul. The multitude,

Tracking them to the secret wood,
Tore limb from limb their innocent child,
And stabbed and trampled on it's mother ;
But the youth, for God's most holy grace,
A priest saved to burn in the market-place.

Duly at evening Helen came
To this lone silent spot,
From the wrecks of a tale of wilder sorrow
So much of sympathy to borrow
As soothed her own dark lot.
Duly each evening from her home,
With her fair child would Helen come
To sit upon that antique seat,
While the hues of day were pale ;
And the bright boy beside her feet
Now lay, lifting at intervals
His broad blue eyes on her ;
Now, where some sudden impulse calls
Following.   He was a gentle boy
And in all gentle sports took joy ;
Oft in a dry leaf for a boat,

With a small feather for a sail,
His fancy on that spring would float,
If some invisible breeze might stir
It's marble calm : and Helen smiled
Thro' tears of awe on the gay child,
To think that a boy as fair as he,
In years which never more may be,
By that same fount, in that same wood,
The like sweet fancies had pursued;
And that a mother, lost like her,
Had mournfully sate watching him.
Then all the scene was wont to swim
Through the mist of a burning tear.

For many months had Helen known
This scene; and now she thither turned
Her footsteps, not alone.
The friend whose falsehood she had mourned,
Sate with her on that seat of stone.
Silent they sate; for evening,
And the power it's glimpses bring
Had, with one awful shadow, quelled

The passion of their grief. They sate
With linked hands, for unrepelled
Had Helen taken Rosalind's.
Like the autumn wind, when it unbinds
The tangled locks of the nightshade's hair,
Which is twined in the sultry summer air
Round the walls of an outworn sepulchre,
Did the voice of Helen, sad and sweet,
And the sound of her heart that ever beat,
As with sighs and words she breathed on her,
Unbind the knots of her friend's despair,
Till her thoughts were free to float and flow;
And from her labouring bosom now,
Like the bursting of a prisoned flame,
The voice of a long pent sorrow came.

ROSALIND.

I saw the dark earth fall upon
The coffin; and I saw the stone
Laid over him whom this cold breast
Had pillowed to his nightly rest!
Thou knowest not, thou can'st not know

My agony.   Oh ! I could not weep:
The sources whence such blessings flow
Were not to be approached by me !
But I could smile, and I could sleep,
Though with a self-accusing heart.
In morning's light, in evening's gloom,
I watched,—and would not thence depart—
My husband's unlamented tomb.
My children knew their sire was gone,
But when I told them,—' he is dead,'—
They laughed aloud in frantic glee,
They clapped their hands and leaped about,
Answering each other's ecstacy
With many a prank and merry shout.
But I sat silent and alone,
Wrapped in the mock of mourning weed.

They laughed, for he was dead : but I
Sate with a hard and tearless eye,
And with a heart which would deny
The secret joy it could not quell,

Low muttering o'er his loathed name;
Till from that self-contention came
Remorse where sin was none; a hell
Which in pure spirits should not dwell.

I'll tell thee truth.   He was a man
Hard, selfish, loving only gold,
Yet full of guile: his pale eyes ran
With tears, which each some falsehood told,
And oft his smooth and bridled tongue
Would give the lie to his flushing cheek:
He was a coward to the strong:
He was a tyrant to the weak,
On whom his vengeance he would wreak:
For scorn, whose arrows search the heart
From many a stranger's eye would dart,
And on his memory cling, and follow
His soul to it's home so cold and hollow.
He was a tyrant to the weak,
And we were such, alas the day!
Oft, when my little ones at play,

Were in youth's natural lightness gay,
Or if they listened to some tale
Of travellers, or of fairy land,—
When the light from the wood-fire's dying
    brand
Flashed on their faces,—if they heard
Or thought they heard upon the stair
His footstep, the suspended word
Died on my lips : we all grew pale :
The babe at my bosom was hushed with fear
If it thought it heard its father near ;
And my two wild boys would near my knee
Cling, cowed and cowering fearfully.

I'll tell thee truth : I loved another.
His name in my ear was ever ringing,
His form to my brain was ever clinging :
Yet if some stranger breathed that name,
My lips turned white, and my heart beat fast :
My nights were once haunted by dreams of
    flame,

C

My days were dim in the shadow cast,
By the memory of the same!
Day and night, day and night,
He was my breath and life and light,
For three short years, which soon were past.
On the fourth, my gentle mother
Led me to the shrine, to be
His sworn bride eternally.
" And now we stood on the altar stair,
When my father came from a distant land,
And with a loud and fearful cry
Rushed between us suddenly.
I saw the stream of his thin grey hair,
I saw his lean and lifted hand,
And heard his words,—and live ! Oh God !
Wherefore do I live ?—' Hold, hold !'
He cried,—' I tell thee 'tis her brother !
Thy mother, boy, beneath the sod
Of yon church-yard rests in her shroud so cold :
I am now weak, and pale, and old :
We were once dear to one another,

I and that corpse! Thou art our child!'
Then with a laugh both long and wild
The youth upon the pavement fell:
They found him dead! All looked on me,
The spasms of my despair to see:
But I was calm. I went away:
I was clammy-cold like clay!
I did not weep: I did not speak:
But day by day, week after week,
I walked about like a corpse alive!
Alas! sweet friend, you must believe
This heart is stone: it did not break.

My father lived a little while,
But all might see that he was dying,
He smiled with such a woful smile!
When he was in the church-yard lying
Among the worms, we grew quite poor,
So that no one would give us bread:
My mother looked at me, and said
Faint words of cheer, which only meant
That she could die and be content;

So I went forth from the same church door
To another husband's bed.
And this was he who died at last,
When weeks and months and years had past,
Through which I firmly did fulfil
My duties, a devoted wife,
With the stern step of vanquished will,
Walking beneath the night of life,
Whose hours extinguished, like slow rain
Falling for ever, pain by pain,
The very hope of death's dear rest;
Which, since the heart within my breast
Of natural life was dispossest,
It's strange sustainer there had been.

When flowers were dead, and grass was green
Upon my mother's grave,—that mother
Whom to outlive, and cheer, and make
My wan eyes glitter for her sake,
Was my vowed task, the single care
Which once gave life to my despair,—

When she was a thing that did not stir
And the crawling worms were cradling her
To a sleep more deep and so more sweet
Than a baby's rocked on its nurse's knee,
I lived : a living pulse then beat
Beneath my heart that awakened me.
What was this pulse so warm and free ?
Alas ! I knew it could not be
My own dull blood : 'twas like a thought
Of liquid love, that spread and wrought
Under my bosom and in my brain,
And crept with the blood through every vein ;
And hour by hour, day after day,
The wonder could not charm away,
But laid in sleep, my wakeful pain,
Until I knew it was a child,
And then I wept.   For long, long years
These frozen eyes had shed no tears :
But now—'twas the season fair and mild
When April has wept itself to May :
I sate through the sweet sunny day

By my window bowered round with leaves,
And down my cheeks the quick tears ran
Like twinkling rain-drops from the eaves,
When warm spring showers are passing o'er :
O Helen, none can ever tell
The joy it was to weep once more !

I wept to think how hard it were
To kill my babe, and take from it
The sense of light, and the warm air,
And my own fond and tender care,
And love and smiles ; ere I knew yet
That these for it might, as for me,
Be the masks of a grinning mockery.
And haply, I would dream, 'twere sweet
To feed it from my faded breast,
Or mark my own heart's restless beat
Rock it to it's untroubled rest,
And watch the growing soul beneath
Dawn in faint smiles ; and hear its breath,
Half interrupted by calm sighs,

And search the depth of its fair eyes
For long departed memories!
And so I lived till that sweet load
Was lightened.   Darkly forward flowed
The stream of years, and on it bore
Two shapes of gladness to my sight;
Two other babes, delightful more
In my lost soul's abandoned night,
Than their own country ships may be
Sailing towards wrecked mariners,
Who cling to the rock of a wintry sea.
For each, as it came, brought soothing tears,
And a loosening warmth, as each one lay
Sucking the sullen milk away
About my frozen heart, did play,
And weaned it, oh how painfully!—
As they themselves were weaned each one
From that sweet food,—even from the thirst
Of death, and nothingness, and rest,
Strange inmate of a living breast!
Which all that I had undergone
Of grief and shame, since she, who first

The gates of that dark refuge closed,
Came to my sight, and almost burst
The seal of that Lethean spring ;
But these fair shadows interposed :
For all delights are shadows now !
And from my brain to my dull brow
The heavy tears gather and flow :
I cannot speak : Oh let me weep !

The tears which fell from her wan eyes
Glimmered among the moonlight dew :
Her deep hard sobs and heavy sighs
Their echoes in the darkness threw.
When she grew calm, she thus did keep
The tenor of her tale :

                    He died :
I know not how : he was not old,
If age be numbered by its years :
But he was bowed and bent with fears,
Pale with the quenchless thirst of gold,
Which, like fierce fever, left him weak

And his strait lip and bloated cheek
Were warped in spasms by hollow sneers;
And selfish cares with barren plough,
Not age, had lined his narrow brow,
And foul and cruel thoughts, which feed
Upon the withering life within,
Like vipers on some poisonous weed.
Whether his ill were death or sin
None knew, until he died indeed,
And then men owned they were the same.

Seven days within my chamber lay
That corse, and my babes made holiday:
At last, I told them what is death:
The eldest, with a kind of shame,
Came to my knees with silent breath,
And sate awe-striken at my feet;
And soon the others left their play,
And sate there too.   It is unmeet
To shed on the brief flower of youth
The withering knowledge of the grave;
From me remorse then wrung that truth.

I could not bear the joy which gave
Too just a response to mine own.
In vain.   I dared not feign a groan ;
And in their artless looks I saw,
Between the mists of fear and awe,
That my own thought was theirs ; and they
Expressed it not in words, but said,
Each in its heart, how every day
Will pass in happy work and play,
Now he is dead and gone away.

After the funeral all our kin
Assembled, and the will was read.
My friend, I tell thee, even the dead
Have strength, their putrid shrouds within,
To blast and torture.   Those who live
Still fear the living, but a corse
Is merciless, and power doth give
To such pale tyrants half the spoil
He rends from those who groan and toil,
Because they blush not with remorse
Among their crawling worms.   Behold,

I have no child! my tale grows old
With grief, and staggers: let it reach
The limits of my feeble speech,
And languidly at length recline
On the brink of its own grave and mine.

Thou knowest what a thing is Poverty
Among the fallen on evil days:
'Tis Crime, and Fear, and Infamy,
And houseless Want in frozen ways
Wandering ungarmented, and Pain,
And, worse than all, that inward stain
Foul Self-contempt, which drowns in sneers
Youth's starlight smile, and makes its tears
First like hot gall, then dry for ever!
And well thou knowest a mother never
Could doom her children to this ill,
And well he knew the same. The will
Imported, that if e'er again
I sought my children to behold,
Or in my birth-place did remain
Beyond three days, whose hours were told,

They should inherit nought : and he,
To whom next came their patrimony,
A sallow lawyer, cruel and cold,
Aye watched me, as the will was read,
With eyes askance, which sought to see
The secrets of my agony;
And with close lips and anxious brow
Stood canvassing still to and fro
The chance of my resolve, and all
The dead man's caution just did call ;
For in that killing lie 'twas said—
" She is adulterous, and doth hold
In secret that the Christian creed
Is false, and therefore is much need
That I should have a care to save
My children from eternal fire."
Friend, he was sheltered by the grave,
And therefore dared to be a liar !
In truth, the Indian on the pyre
Of her dead husband, half consumed,
As well might there be false, as I
To those abhorred embraces doomed,

Far worse than fire's brief agony.
As to the Christian creed, if true
Or false, I never questioned it :
I took it as the vulgar do :
Nor my vext soul had leisure yet
To doubt the things men say, or deem
That they are other than they seem.

All present who those crimes did hear,
In feigned or actual scorn and fear,
Men, women, children, slunk away,
Whispering with self-contented pride,
Which half suspects its own base lie.
I spoke to none, nor did abide,
But silently I went my way,
Nor noticed I where joyously
Sate my two younger babes at play,
In the court-yard through which I past;
But went with footsteps firm and fast
Till I came to the brink of the ocean green,
And there, a woman with grey hairs,
Who had my mother's servant been,

Kneeling, with many tears and prayers,
Made me accept a purse of gold,
Half of the earnings she had kept
To refuge her when weak and old.

With woe, which never sleeps or slept,
I wander now.   'Tis a vain thought—
But on yon alp, whose snowy head
'Mid the azure air is islanded,
(We see it o'er the flood of cloud,
Which sunrise from its eastern caves
Drives, wrinkling into golden waves,
Hung with its precipices proud,
From that grey stone where first we met)
There, now who knows the dead feel nought?
Should be my grave; for he who yet
Is my soul's soul, once said : " 'Twere sweet
'Mid stars and lightnings to abide,
And winds and lulling snows, that beat
With their soft flakes the mountain wide,
When weary meteor lamps repose,
And languid storms their pinions close:

And all things strong and bright and pure,
And ever during, aye endure :
Who knows, if one were buried there,
But these things might our spirits make,
Amid the all-surrounding air,
Their own eternity partake ? "
Then 'twas a wild and playful saying
At which I laughed, or seemed to laugh :
They were his words: now heed my praying,
And let them be my epitaph.
Thy memory for a term may be
My monument.   Wilt remember me ?
I know thou wilt, and canst forgive
Whilst in this erring world to live
My soul disdained not, that I thought
Its lying forms were worthy aught
And much less thee.

HELEN.

O speak not so,
But come to me and pour thy woe
Into this heart, full though it be,

Aye overflowing with its own :
I thought that grief had severed me
From all beside who weep and groan ;
Its likeness upon earth to be,
Its express image; but thou art
More wretched.   Sweet ! we will not part
Henceforth, if death be not division ;
If so, the dead feel no contrition.
But wilt thou hear since last we parted
All that has left me broken hearted ?

ROSALIND.

Yes, speak. The faintest stars are scarcely shorn
Of their thin beams by that delusive morn
Which sinks again in darkness, like the light
Of early love, soon lost in total night.

HELEN.

Alas ! Italian winds are mild,
But my bosom is cold—wintry cold—
When the warm air weaves, among the fresh
         leaves,

Soft music, my poor brain is wild,
And I am weak like a nursling child,
Though my soul with grief is gray and old.

ROSALIND.

Weep not at thine own words, though they
    must make
Me weep.   What is thy tale ?

HELEN.

      I fear 'twill shake
Thy gentle heart with tears.   Thou well
Rememberest when we met no more,
And, though I dwelt with Lionel,
That friendless caution pierced me sore
With grief; a wound my spirit bore
Indignantly, but when he died
With him lay dead both hope and pride.

Alas ! all hope is buried now.
But then men dreamed the aged earth
Was labouring in that mighty birth,

D

Which many a poet and a sage
Has aye foreseen—the happy age
When truth and love shall dwell below
Among the works and ways of men ;
Which on this world not power but will
Even now is wanting to fulfil.

Among mankind what thence befel
Of strife, how vain, is known too well;
When liberty's dear pæan fell
'Mid murderous howls.   To Lionel,
Though of great wealth and lineage high,
Yet through those dungeon walls there came
Thy thrilling light, O liberty !
And as the meteor's midnight flame
Startles the dreamer, sun-like truth
Flashed on his visionary youth,
And filled him, not with love, but faith,
And hope, and courage mute in death ;
For love and life in him were twins,
Born at one birth : in every other
First life then love its course begins,

Though they be children of one mother;
And so through this dark world they fleet
Divided, till in death they meet:
But he loved all things ever. Then
He past amid the strife of men,
And stood at the throne of armed power
Pleading for a world of woe:
Secure as one on a rock-built tower
O'er the wrecks which the surge trails to and fro,
'Mid the passions wild of human kind
He stood, like a spirit calming them;
For, it was said, his words could bind
Like music the lulled crowd, and stem
That torrent of unquiet dream,
Which mortals truth and reason deem,
But is revenge and fear and pride.
Joyous he was; and hope and peace
On all who heard him did abide,
Raining like dew from his sweet talk,
As where the evening star may walk
Along the brink of the gloomy seas,
Liquid mists of splendour quiver.

His very gestures touched to tears
The unpersuaded tyrant, never
So moved before : his presence stung
The torturers with their victim's pain,
And none knew how ; and through their ear
The subtle witchcraft of his tongue
Unlocked the hearts of those who keep
Gold, the world's bond of slavery.
Men wondered, and some sneered to see
One sow what he could never reap :
For he is rich, they said, and young,
And might drink from the depths of luxury.
If he seeks fame, fame never crowned
The champion of a trampled creed :
If he seeks power, power is enthroned
'Mid antient rights and wrongs, to feed
Which hungry wolves with praise and spoil,
Those who would sit near power must toil ;
And such, there sitting, all may see.
What seeks he ?   All that others seek
He casts away, like a vile weed
Which the sea casts unreturningly.

That poor and hungry men should break
The laws which wreak them toil and scorn,
We understand ; but Lionel
We know is rich and nobly born.
So wondered they: yet all men loved
Young Lionel, though few approved ;
All but the priests, whose hatred fell
Like the unseen blight of a smiling day,
The withering honey dew, which clings
Under the bright green buds of May,
Whilst they unfold their emerald wings:
For he made verses wild and queer
On the strange creeds priests hold so dear,
Because they bring them land and gold.
Of devils and saints and all such gear,
He made tales which whoso heard or read
Would laugh till he were almost dead.
So this grew a proverb : "don't get old
Till Lionel's ' banquet in hell' you hear,
And then you will laugh yourself young again."
So the priests hated him, and he
Repaid their hate with cheerful glee.

Ah, smiles and joyance quickly died,
For public hope grew pale and dim
In an altered time and tide,
And in its wasting withered him,
As a summer flower that blows too soon
Droops in the smile of the waning moon,
When it scatters through an April night
The frozen dews of wrinkling blight.
None now hoped more.   Grey Power was seated
Safely on her ancestral throne;
And Faith, the Python, undefeated,
Even to its blood-stained steps dragged on
Her foul and wounded train, and men
Were trampled and deceived again,
And words and shews again could bind
The wailing tribes of human kind
In scorn and famine.   Fire and blood
Raged round the raging multitude,
To fields remote by tyrants sent
To be the scorned instrument
With which they drag from mines of gore
The chains their slaves yet ever wore :

And in the streets men met each other,
And by old altars and in halls,
And smiled again at festivals.
But each man found in his heart's brother
Cold cheer; for all, though half deceived,
The outworn creeds again believed,
And the same round anew began,
Which the weary world yet ever ran.

Many then wept, not tears, but gall
Within their hearts, like drops which fall
Wasting the fountain-stone away.
And in that dark and evil day
Did all desires and thoughts, that claim
Men's care—ambition, friendship, fame,
Love, hope, though hope was now despair—
Induc the colours of this change,
As from the all-surrounding air
The earth takes hues obscure and strange,
When storm and earthquake linger there.

And so, my friend, it then befel
To many, most to Lionel,

Whose hope was like the life of youth
Within him, and when dead, became
A spirit of unresting flame,
Which goaded him in his distress
Over the world's vast wilderness.
Three years he left his native land,
And on the fourth, when he returned,
None knew him : he was striken deep
With some disease of mind, and turned
Into aught unlike Lionel.
On him, on whom, did he pause in sleep,
Serenest smiles were wont to keep,
And, did he wake, a winged band
Of bright persuasions, which had fed
On his sweet lips and liquid eyes,
Kept their swift pinions half outspread,
To do on men his least command ;
On him, whom once 'twas paradise
Even to behold, now misery lay :
In his own heart 'twas merciless,
To all things else none may express
Its innocence and tenderness.

'Twas said that he had refuge sought
In love from his unquiet thought
In distant lands, and been deceived
By some strange shew ; for there were found,
Blotted with tears as those relieved
By their own words are wont to do,
These mournful verses on the ground,
By all who read them blotted too.

" How am I changed ! my hopes were once like
    fire :
1 loved, and I believed that life was love.
How am I lost ! on wings of swift desire
Among Heaven's winds my spirit once did move.
I slept, and silver dreams did aye inspire
My liquid sleep: I woke, and did approve
All nature to my heart, and thought to make
A paradise of earth for one sweet sake.

" I love, but I believe in love no more.
I feel desire, but hope not. O, from sleep

Most vainly must my weary brain implore
Its long lost flattery now : I wake to weep,
And sit through the long day gnawing the core
Of my bitter heart, and, like a miser, keep,
Since none in what I feel take pain or plea-
    sure,
To my own soul its self-consuming treasure."

He dwelt beside me near the sea :
And oft in evening did we meet,
When the waves, beneath the starlight, flee
O'er the yellow sands with silver feet,
And talked : our talk was sad and sweet,
Till slowly from his mien there passed
The desolation which it spoke ;
And smiles,—as when the lightning's blast
Has parched some heaven-delighting oak,
The next spring shews leaves pale and rare,
But like flowers delicate and fair,
On its rent boughs,—again arrayed
His countenance in tender light :

His words grew subtile fire, which made
The air his hearers breathed delight :
His motions, like the winds, were free,
Which bend the bright grass gracefully,
Then fade away in circlets faint :
And winged hope, on which upborne
His soul seemed hovering in his eyes,
Like some bright spirit newly born
Floating amid the sunny skies,
Sprang forth from his rent heart anew.
Yet o'er his talk, and looks, and mien,
Tempering their loveliness too keen,
Past woe its shadow backward threw,
Till like an exhalation, spread
From flowers half drunk with evening dew,
They did become infectious : sweet
And subtile mists of sense and thought :
Which wrapt us soon, when we might meet,
Almost from our own looks and aught
The wide world holds. And so, his mind
Was healed, while mine grew sick with fear :
For ever now his health declined,

Like some frail bark which cannot bear
The impulse of an altered wind,
Though prosperous: and my heart grew full
'Mid its new joy of a new care :
For his cheek became, not pale, but fair,
As rose-o'ershadowed lilies are ;
And soon his deep and sunny hair,
In this alone less beautiful,
Like grass in tombs grew wild and rare.
The blood in his translucent veins
Beat, not like animal life, but love
Seemed now its sullen springs to move,
When life had failed, and all its pains :
And sudden sleep would seize him oft
Like death, so calm, but that a tear,
His pointed eye-lashes between,
Would gather in the light serene
Of smiles, whose lustre bright and soft
Beneath lay undulating there.
His breath was like inconstant flame,
As eagerly it went and came ;
And I hung o'er him in his sleep,

Till, like an image in the lake
Which rains disturb, my tears would break
The shadow of that slumber deep :
Then he would bid me not to weep,
And say with flattery false, yet sweet,
That death and he could never meet, .
If I would never part with him.
And so we loved, and did unite
All that in us was yet divided :
For when he said, that many a rite,
By men to bind but once provided,
Could not be shared by him and me,
Or they would kill him in their glee,
I shuddered, and then laughing said—
" We will have rites our faith to bind,
But our church shall be the starry night,
Our altar the grassy earth outspread,
And our priest the muttering wind."

'Twas sunset as I spoke : one star
Had scarce burst forth, when from afar

The ministers of misrule sent,
Seized upon Lionel, and bore
His chained limbs to a dreary tower,
In the midst of a city vast and wide.
For he, they said, from his mind had bent
Against their gods keen blasphemy,
For which, though his soul must roasted be
In hell's red lakes immortally
Yet even on earth must he abide
The vengeance of their slaves : a trial,
I think, men call it.   What avail
Are prayers and tears, which chase denial
From the fierce savage, nursed in hate ?
What the knit soul that pleading and pale
Makes wan the quivering cheek, which late
It painted with its own delight ?
We were divided.   As I could,
I stilled the tingling of my blood,
And followed him in their despite,
As a widow follows, pale and wild,
The murderers and corse of her only child ;

And when we came to the prison door
And I prayed to share his dungeon floor
With prayers which rarely have been spurned,
And when men drove me forth and I
Stared with blank frenzy on the sky,
A farewell look of love he turned,
Half calming me; then gazed awhile,
As if thro' that black and massy pile,
And thro' the crowd around him there,
And thro' the dense and murky air,
And the thronged streets, he did espy
What poets know and prophecy;
And said, with voice that made them shiver
And clung like music in my brain,
And which the mute walls spoke again
Prolonging it with deepened strain:
" Fear not, the tyrants shall rule for ever,
Or the priests of the bloody faith;
They stand on the brink of that mighty river,
Whose waves they have tainted with death:
It is fed from the depths of a thousand dells,
Around them it foams, and rages, and swells,

And their swords and their sceptres I floating
    see,
Like wrecks in the surge of eternity."

I dwelt beside the prison gate,
And the strange crowd that out and in
Passed, some, no doubt, with mine own fate,
Might have fretted me with its ceaseless din,
But the fever of care was louder within.
Soon, but too late, in penitence
Or fear, his foes released him thence :
I saw his thin and languid form,
As leaning on the jailor's arm,
Whose hardened eyes grew moist the while,
To meet his mute and faded smile,
And hear his words of kind farewell,
He tottered forth from his damp cell.
Many had never wept before,
From whom fast tears then gushed and fell :
Many will relent no more,
Who sobbed like infants then : aye, all
Who thronged the prison's stony hall,

The rulers or the slaves of law,
Felt with a new surprise and awe
That they were human, till strong shame
Made them again become the same.
The prison blood-hounds, huge and grim,
From human looks the infection caught,
And fondly crouched and fawned on him;
And men have heard the prisoners say,
Who in their rotting dungeons lay;
That from that hour, throughout one day,
The fierce despair and hate which kept
Their trampled bosoms almost slept :
When, like twin vultures, they hung feeding
On each heart's wound, wide torn and bleeding,
Because their jailors' rule, they thought,
Grew merciful, like a parent's sway.

I know not how, but we were free :
And Lionel sate alone with me,
As the carriage drove thro' the streets apace ;
And we looked upon each other's face ;
And the blood in our fingers intertwined

E

Ran like the thoughts of a single mind,
As the swift emotions went and came
Thro' the veins of each united frame.
So thro' the long long streets we past
Of the million-peopled City vast;
Which is that desart, where each one
Seeks his mate yet is alone,
Beloved and sought and mourned of none;
Until the clear blue sky was seen,
And the grassy meadows bright and green,
And then I sunk in his embrace,
Enclosing there a mighty space
Of love: and so we travelled on
By woods, and fields of yellow flowers,
And towns, and villages, and towers,
Day after day of happy hours.
It was the azure time of June,
When the skies are deep in the stainless noon,
And the warm and fitful breezes shake
The fresh green leaves of the hedge-row briar,
And there were odours then to make
The very breath we did respire

A liquid element, whereon
Our spirits, like delighted things
That walk the air on subtle wings,
Floated and mingled far away,
'Mid the warm winds of the sunny day.
And when the evening star came forth
Above the curve of the new bent moon,
And light and sound ebbed from the earth,
Like the tide of the full and weary sea
To the depths of its tranquillity,
Our natures to its own repose
Did the earth's breathless sleep attune :
Like flowers, which on each other close
Their languid leaves when day-light's gone,
We lay, till new emotions came,
Which seemed to make each mortal frame
One soul of interwoven flame,
A life in life, a second birth
In worlds diviner far than earth,
Which, like two strains of harmony
That mingle in the silent sky
Then slowly disunite, past by

And left the tenderness of tears,
A soft oblivion of all fears,
A sweet sleep: so we travelled on
Till we came to the home of Lionel,
Among the mountains wild and lone,
Beside the hoary western sea,
Which near the verge of the echoing shore
The massy forest shadowed o'er.

The ancient steward, with hair all hoar,
As we alighted, wept to see
His master changed so fearfully;
And the old man's sobs did waken me
From my dream of unremaining gladness;
The truth flashed o'er me like quick madness
When I looked, and saw that there was death
On Lionel: yet day by day
He lived, till fear grew hope and faith,
And in my soul I dared to say,
Nothing so bright can pass away:
Death is dark, and foul, and dull,
But he is—O how beautiful!

Yet day by day he grew more weak,
And his sweet voice, when he might speak,
Which ne'er was loud, became more low ;
And the light which flashed through his waxen
    cheek
Grew faint, as the rose-like hues which flow
From sunset o'er the Alpine snow :
And death seemed not like death in him,
For the spirit of life o'er every limb
Lingered, a mist of sense and thought.
When the summer wind faint odours brought
From mountain flowers, even as it passed
His cheek would change, as the noon-day sea
Which the dying breeze sweeps fitfully.
If but a cloud the sky o'ercast,
You might see his colour come and go,
And the softest strain of music made
Sweet smiles, yet sad, arise and fade
Amid the dew of his tender eyes ;
And the breath, with intermitting flow,
Made his pale lips quiver and part.
You might hear the beatings of his heart,

Quick, but not strong; and with my tresses
When oft he playfully would bind
In the bowers of mossy lonelinesses
His neck, and win me so to mingle
In the sweet depth of woven caresses,
And our faint limbs were intertwined,
Alas! the unquiet life did tingle
From mine own heart through every vein,
Like a captive in dreams of liberty,
Who beats the walls of his stony cell.
But his, it seemed already free,
Like the shadow of fire surrounding me!
On my faint eyes and limbs did dwell
That spirit as it passed, till soon,
As a frail cloud wandering o'er the moon,
Beneath its light invisible,
Is seen when it folds its grey wings again
To alight on midnight's dusky plain,
I lived and saw, and the gathering soul
Passed from beneath that strong controul,
And I fell on a life which was sick with fear
Of all the woe that now I bear.

Amid a bloomless myrtle wood,
On a green and sea-girt promontory,
Not far from where we dwelt, there stood
In record of a sweet sad story,
An altar and a temple bright
Circled by steps, and o'er the gate
Was sculptured, " To Fidelity
And in the shrine an image sate,
All veiled : but there was seen the light
Of smiles, which faintly could express
A mingled pain and tenderness
Through that ethereal drapery.
The left hand held the head, the right—
Beyond the veil, beneath the skin,
You might see the nerves quivering within—
Was forcing the point of a barbed dart,
Into its side-convulsing heart.
An unskilled hand, yet one informed
With genius, had the marble warmed
With that pathetic life. This tale
It told : A dog had from the sea,
When the tide was raging fearfully,

Dragged Lionel's mother, weak and pale,
Then died beside her on the sand,
And she that temple thence had planned ;
But it was Lionel's own hand
Had wrought the image.   Each new moon
That lady did, in this lone fane,
The rites of a religion sweet,
Whose god was in her heart and brain :
The seasons' loveliest flowers were strewn
On the marble floor beneath her feet,
And she brought crowns of sea-buds white,
Whose odour is so sweet and faint,
And weeds, like branching chrysolyte,
Woven in devices fine and quaint,
And tears from her brown eyes did stain
The altar : need but look upon
That dying statue fair and wan,
If tears should cease, to weep again :
And rare Arabian odours came,
Through the myrtle copses steaming thence
From the hissing frankincense,
Whose smoke, wool-white as ocean foam,

Hung in dense flocks beneath the dome,
That ivory dome, whose azure night
With golden stars, like heaven, was bright
O'er the split cedars pointed flame ;
And the lady's harp would kindle there
The melody of an old air,
Softer than sleep ; the villagers
Mixt their religion up with her's,
And as they listened round, shed tears.

One eve he led me to this fane :
Daylight on its last purple cloud
Was lingering grey, and soon her strain
The nightingale began ; now loud,
Climbing in circles the windless sky,
Now dying music ; suddenly
'Tis scattered in a thousand notes,
And now to the hushed ear it floats
Like field smells known in infancy,
Then failing, soothes the air again.
We sate within that temple lone,
Pavilioned round with Parian stone :

His mother's harp stood near, and oft
I had awakened music soft
Amid its wires: the nightingale
Was pausing in her heaven-taught tale:
" Now drain the cup," said Lionel,
" Which the poet-bird has crowned so well
With the wine of her bright and liquid song !
Heardst thou not sweet words among
That heaven-resounding minstrelsy ?
Heardst thou not, that those who die
Awake in a world of extacy ?
That love, when limbs are interwoven,
And sleep, when the night of life is cloven,
And thought, to the world's dim boundaries
          clinging,
And music, when one beloved is singing,
Is death ?   Let us drain right joyously
The cup which the sweet bird fills for me."
He paused, and to my lips he bent
His own : like spirit his words went
Through all my limbs with the speed of fire ;
And his keen eyes, glittering through mine,

Filled me with the flame divine,
Which in their orbs was burning far,
Like the light of an unmeasured star,
In the sky of midnight dark and deep :
Yes, 'twas his soul that did inspire
Sounds, which my skill could ne'er awaken ;
And first, I felt my fingers sweep
The harp, and a long quivering cry
Burst from my lips in symphony :
The dusk and solid air was shaken,
As swift and swifter the notes came
From my touch, that wandered like quick flame.
And from my bosom, labouring
With some unutterable thing :
The awful sound of my own voice made
My faint lips tremble, in some mood
Of wordless thought Lionel stood
So pale, that even beside his cheek
The snowy column from its shade
Caught whiteness : yet his countenance
Raised upward, burned with radiance
Of spirit-piercing joy, whose light,

Like the moon struggling through the night
Of whirlwind-rifted clouds, did break
With beams that might not be confined.
I paused, but soon his gestures kindled
New power, as by the moving wind
The waves are lifted, and my song
To low soft notes now changed and dwindled,
And from the twinkling wires among,
My languid fingers drew and flung
Circles of life dissolving sound,
Yet faint: in aery rings they bound
My Lionel, who, as every strain
Grew fainter but more sweet, his mien
Sunk with the sound relaxedly;
And slowly now he turned to me,
As slowly faded from his face
That awful joy: with looks serene
He was soon drawn to my embrace,
And my wild song then died away
In murmurs: words, I dare not say
We mixed, and on his lips mine fed
Till they methought felt still and cold:

"What is it with thee, love?" I said:
No word, no look, no motion! yes,
There was a change, but spare to guess,
Nor let that moment's hope be told.
I looked, and knew that he was dead,
And fell, as the eagle on the plain
Falls when life deserts her brain,
And the mortal lightning is veiled again.

O that I were now dead! but such
Did they not, love, demand too much
Those dying murmurs? He forbade.
O that I once again were mad!
And yet, dear Rosalind, not so,
For I would live to share thy woe.
Sweet boy, did I forget thee too?
Alas, we know not what we do
When we speak words.

No memory more
Is in my mind of that sea shore.
Madness came on me, and a troop

Of misty shapes did seem to sit
Beside me, on a vessel's poop,
And the clear north wind was driving it.
Then I heard strange tongues, and saw strange
       flowers,
And the stars methought grew unlike ours,
And the azure sky and the stormless sea
Made me believe that I had died,
And waked in a world, which was to me
Drear hell, though heaven to all beside :
Then a dead sleep fell on my mind,
Whilst animal life many long years
Had rescued from a chasm of tears ;
And when I woke, I wept to find
That the same lady, bright and wise,
With silver locks and quick brown eyes,
The mother of my Lionel,
Had tended me in my distress,
And died some months before.   Nor less
Wonder, but far more peace and joy
Brought in that hour my lovely boy;
For through that trance my soul had well

The impress of thy being kept ;
And if I waked, or if I slept,
No doubt, though memory faithless be,
Thy image ever dwelt on me ;
And thus, O Lionel, like thee
Is our sweet child.   'Tis sure most strange
I knew not of so great a change,
As that which gave him birth, who now
Is all the solace of my woe.

That Lionel great wealth had left
By will to me, and that of all
The ready lies of law bereft,
My child and me might well befall.
But let me think not of the scorn,
Which from the meanest I have borne,
When, for my child's beloved sake,
I mixed with slaves, to vindicate
The very laws themselves do make :
Let me not say scorn is my fate,
Lest I be proud, suffering the same
With those who live in deathless fame.

She ceased.—" Lo, where red morning thro'
    the woods
Is burning o'er the dew ;" said Rosalind.
And with these words they rose, and towards
    the flood
Of the blue lake, beneath the leaves now wind
With equal steps and fingers intertwined :
Thence to a lonely dwelling, where the shore
Is shadowed with steep rocks, and cypresses
Cleave with their dark green cones the silent
    skies,
And with their shadows the clear depths below,
And where a little terrace from its bowers,
Of blooming myrtle and faint lemon-flowers,
Scatters its sense-dissolving fragrance o'er
The liquid marble of the windless lake ;
And where the aged forest's limbs look hoar,
Under the leaves which their green garments
    make,
They come : 'tis Helen's home, and clean and
    white,
Like one which tyrants spare on our own land

In some such solitude, its casements bright
Shone thro' their vine-leaves in the morning
    sun,
And even within 'twas scarce like Italy.
And when she saw how all things there were
    planned,
As in an English home, dim memory
Disturbed poor Rosalind : she stood as one
Whose mind is where his body cannot be,
Till Helen led her where her child yet slept,
And said, " Observe, that brow was Lionel's,
Those lips were his, and so he ever kept
One arm in sleep, pillowing his head with it.
You cannot see his eyes, they are two wells
Of liquid love : let us not wake him yet."
But Rosalind could bear no more, and wept
A shower of burning tears, which fell upon
His face, and so his opening lashes shone
With tears unlike his own, as he did leap
In sudden wonder from his innocent sleep.

So Rosalind and Helen lived together

F

Thenceforth, changed in all else, yet friends
    again,
Such as they were, when o'er the mountain
    heather
They wandered in their youth, through sun and
    rain.
And after many years, for human things
Change even like the ocean and the wind,
Her daughter was restored to Rosalind,
And in their circle thence some visitings
Of joy 'mid their new calm would intervene :
A lovely child she was, of looks serene,
And motions which o'er things indifferent shed
The grace and gentleness from whence they
    came.
And Helen's boy grew with her, and they fed
From the same flowers of thought, until each
    mind
Like springs which mingle in one flood became,
And in their union soon their parents saw
The shadow of the peace denied to them.
And Rosalind, for when the living stem

Is cankered in its heart, the tree must fall,
Died ere her time; and with deep grief and awe
The pale survivors followed her remains
Beyond the region of dissolving rains,
Up the cold mountain she was wont to call
Her tomb; and on Chiavenna's precipice
They raised a pyramid of lasting ice,
Whose polished sides, ere day had yet begun,
Caught the first glow of the unrisen sun,
The last, when it had sunk; and thro' the night
The charioteers of Arctos wheeled round
Its glittering point, as seen from Helen's home,
Whose sad inhabitants each year would come,
With willing steps climbing that rugged height,
And hang long locks of hair, and garlands bound
With amaranth flowers, which, in the clime's
            despite,
Filled the frore air with unaccustomed light:
Such flowers, as in the wintry memory bloom
Of one friend left, adorned that frozen tomb.

Helen, whose spirit was of softer mould,

Whose sufferings too were less, death slowlier
    led
Into the peace of his dominion cold :
She died among her kindred, being old.
And know, that if love die not in the dead
As in the living, none of mortal kind
Are blest, as now Helen and Rosalind.

LINES

WRITTEN AMONG THE EUGANEAN HILLS,

OCTOBER, 1818.

MANY a green isle needs must be
In the deep wide sea of misery,
Or the mariner, worn and wan,
Never thus could voyage on
Day and night, and night and day,
Drifting on his dreary way,
With the solid darkness black
Closing round his vessel's track ;
Whilst above the sunless sky,
Big with clouds, hangs heavily,
And behind the tempest fleet
Hurries on with lightning feet,
Riving sail, and cord, and plank,
Till the ship has almost drank

Death from the o'er-brimming deep ;
And sinks down, down, like that sleep
When the dreamer seems to be
Weltering through eternity ;
And the dim low line before
Of a dark and distant shore
Still recedes, as ever still
Longing with divided will,
But no power to seek or shun,
He is ever drifted on
O'er the unreposing wave
To the haven of the grave.
What, if there no friends will greet ;
What, if there no heart will meet
His with love's impatient beat ;
Wander wheresoe'er he may,
Can he dream before that day
To find refuge from distress
In friendship's smile, in love's caress ?
Then 'twill wreak him little woe
Whether such there be or no :
Senseless is the breast, and cold,

Which relenting love would fold ;
Bloodless are the veins and chill
Which the pulse of pain did fill ;
Every little living nerve
That from bitter words did swerve
Round the tortured lips and brow,
Are like sapless leaflets now
Frozen upon December's bough.
On the beach of a northern sea
Which tempests shake eternally,
As once the wretch there lay to sleep,
Lies a solitary heap,
One white skull and seven dry bones,
On the margin of the stones,
Where a few grey rushes stand,
Boundaries of the sea and land :
Nor is heard one voice of wail
But the sea-mews, as they sail
O'er the billows of the gale ;
Or the whirlwind up and down
Howling, like a slaughtered town,
When a king in glory rides

Through the pomp of fratricides :
Those unburied bones around
There is many a mournful sound ;
There is no lament for him,
Like a sunless vapour, dim,
Who once clothed with life and thought
What now moves nor murmurs not.

Aye, many flowering islands lie
In the waters of wide Agony :
To such a one this morn was led,
My bark by soft winds piloted :
 Mid the mountains Euganean
I stood listening to the pæan,
With which the legioned rooks did hail
The sun's uprise majestical ;
Gathering round with wings all hoar,
Thro' the dewy mist they soar
Like grey shades, till th' eastern heaven
Bursts, and then, as clouds of even,
Flecked with fire and azure, lie
In the unfathomable sky

So their plumes of purple grain,
Starred with drops of golden rain,
Gleam above the sunlight woods,
As in silent multitudes
On the morning's fitful gale
Thro' the broken mist they sail,
And the vapours cloven and gleaming
Follow down the dark steep streaming,
Till all is bright, and clear, and still,
Round the solitary hill.

Beneath is spread like a green sea
The waveless plain of Lombardy,
Bounded by the vaporous air,
Islanded by cities fair;
Underneath day's azure eyes
Ocean's nursling, Venice lies,
A peopled labyrinth of walls,
Amphitrite's destined halls,
Which her hoary sire now paves
With his blue and beaming waves.
Lo ! the sun upsprings behind,

Broad, red, radiant, half reclined
On the level quivering line
Of the waters chrystalline;
And before that chasm of light,
As within a furnace bright,
Column, tower, and dome, and spire,
Shine like obelisks of fire,
Pointing with inconstant motion
From the altar of dark ocean
To the sapphire-tinted skies;
As the flames of sacrifice
From the marble shrines did rise,
As to pierce the dome of gold
Where Apollo spoke of old.

Sun-girt City, thou hast been
Ocean's child, and then his queen;
Now is come a darker day,
And thou soon must be his prey,
If the power that raised thee here
Hallow so thy watery bier.
A less drear ruin then than now,

With thy conquest-branded brow
Stooping to the slave of slaves
From thy throne, among the waves
Wilt thou be, when the sea-mew
Flies, as once before it flew,
O'er thine isles depopulate,
And all is in its antient state,
Save where many a palace gate
With green sea-flowers overgrown
Like a rock of ocean's own,
Topples o'er the abandoned sea
As the tides change sullenly.
The fisher on his watery way,
Wandering at the close of day,
Will spread his sail and seize his oar
Till he pass the gloomy shore,
Lest thy dead should, from their sleep
Bursting o'er the starlight deep,
Lead a rapid masque of death
O'er the waters of his path.

Those who alone thy towers behold
Quivering through aerial gold,

As I now behold them here,
Would imagine not they were
Sepulchres, where human forms,
Like pollution-nourished worms
To the corpse of greatness cling,
Murdered, and now mouldering :
But if Freedom should awake
In her omnipotence, and shake
From the Celtic Anarch's hold
All the keys of dungeons cold,
Where a hundred cities lie
Chained like thee, ingloriously,
Thou and all thy sister band
Might adorn this sunny land,
Twining memories of old time
With new virtues more sublime ;
If not, perish thou and they,
Clouds which stain truth's rising day
By her sun consumed away,
Earth can spare ye : while like flowers,
In the waste of years and hours,
From your dust new nations spring
With more kindly blossoming.

Perish! let there only be
Floating o'er thy hearthless sea,
As the garment of thy sky
Clothes the world immortally,
One remembrance, more sublime
Than the tattered pall of time,
Which scarce hides thy visage wan;
That a tempest-cleaving swan
Of the songs of Albion,
Driven from his ancestral streams
By the might of evil dreams,
Found a nest in thee; and Ocean
Welcomed him with such emotion
That its joy grew his, and sprung
From his lips like music flung
O'er a mighty thunder-fit,
Chastening terror: what though yet
Poesy's unfailing river,
Which thro' Albion winds for ever,
Lashing with melodious wave
Many a sacred poet's grave,
Mourn its latest nursling fled!

What though thou with all thy dead
Scarce can for this fame repay
Aught thine own,—oh, rather say,
Though thy sins and slaveries foul
Overcloud a sunlike soul !
As the ghost of Homer clings
Round Scamander's wasting springs ;
As divinest Shakespeare's might
Fills Avon and the world with light
Like omniscient power, which he
Imaged 'mid mortality ;
As the love from Petrarch's urn,
Yet amid yon hills doth burn,
A quenchless lamp, by which the heart
Sees things unearthly ; so thou art,
Mighty spirit : so shall be
The city that did refuge thee.

Lo, the sun floats up the sky
Like thought-winged Liberty,
Till the universal light
Seems to level plain and height ;

From the sea a mist has spread,
And the beams of morn lie dead
On the towers of Venice now,
Like its glory long ago.
By the skirts of that grey cloud
Many-domed Padua proud
Stands, a peopled solitude,
'Mid the harvest shining plain,
Where the peasant heaps his grain
In the garner of his foe,
And the milk-white oxen slow
With the purple vintage strain,
Heaped upon the creaking wain,
That the brutal Celt may swill
Drunken sleep with savage will ;
And the sickle to the sword
Lies unchanged, though many a lord,
Like a weed whose shade is poison,
Overgrows this region's foizon,
Sheaves of whom are ripe to come
To destruction's harvest home :
Men must reap the things they sow,

Force from force must ever flow,
Or worse; but 'tis a bitter woe
That love or reason cannot change
The despot's rage, the slave's revenge.

Padua, thou within whose walls
Those mute guests at festivals,
Son and Mother, Death and Sin,
Played at dice for Ezzelin,
Till Death cried, " I win, I win ! "
And Sin cursed to lose the wager,
But Death promised, to assuage her,
That he would petition for
Her to be made Vice-Emperor,
When the destined years were o'er,
Over all between the Po
And the eastern Alpine snow,
Under the mighty Austrian.
Sin smiled so as Sin only can,
And since that time, aye, long before,
Both have ruled from shore to shore,

Tyrants as the sun the swallow,
As Repentance follows Crime,
And as changes follow Time.

In thine halls the lamp of learning,
Padua, now no more is burning;
Like a meteor, whose wild way
Is lost over the grave of day,
It gleams betrayed and to betray;
Once remotest nations came
To adore that sacred flame,
When it lit not many a hearth
On this cold and gloomy earth:
Now new fires from antique light
Spring beneath the wide world's might;
But their spark lies dead in thee,
Trampled out by tyranny.
As the Norway woodman quells,
In the depth of piny dells,
One light flame among the brakes
While the boundless forest shakes,
And its mighty trunks are torn

G

By the fire thus lowly born :
The spark beneath his feet is dead,
He starts to see the flames it fed
Howling through the darkened sky
With a myriad tongues victoriously,
And sinks down in fear : so thou,
O tyranny, beholdest now
Light around thee, and thou hearest
The loud flames ascend, and fearest :
Grovel on the earth : aye, hide
In the dust thy purple pride !

Noon descends around me now :
'Tis the noon of autumn's glow,
When a soft and purple mist
Like a vaporous amethyst,
Or an air-dissolved star
Mingling light and fragrance, far
From the curved horizon's bound
To the point of heaven's profound,
Fills the overflowing sky ;
And the plains that silent lie

Underneath, the leaves unsodden
Where the infant frost has trodder
With his morning-winged feet,
Whose bright print is gleaming yet;
And the red and golden vines,
Piercing with their trellised lines
The rough, dark-skirted wilderness;
The dun and bladed grass no less,
Pointing from this hoary tower
In the windless air; the flower
Glimmering at my feet; the line
Of the olive-sandalled Apennine
In the south dimly islanded;
And the Alps, whose snows are spread
High between the clouds and sun;
And of living things each one;
And my spirit which so long
Darkened this swift stream of song,
Interpenetrated lie
By the glory of the sky:
Be it love, light, harmony,
Odour, or the soul of all

Which from heaven like dew doth fall,
Or the mind which feeds this verse
Peopling the lone universe.

Noon descends, and after noon
Autumn's evening meets me soon,
Leading the infantine moon,
And that one star, which to her
Almost seems to minister
Half the crimson light she brings
From the sunset's radiant springs:
And the soft dreams of the morn,
(Which like winged winds had borne
To that silent isle, which lies
'Mid remembered agonies,
The frail bark of this lone being,)
Pass, to other sufferers fleeing,
And its antient pilot, Pain,
Sits beside the helm again.

Other flowering isles must be
In the sea of life and agony:

Other spirits float and flee
O'er that gulph : even now, perhaps,
On some rock the wild wave wraps,
With folded wings they waiting sit
For my bark, to pilot it
To some calm and blooming cove,
Where for me, and those I love,
May a windless bower be built,
Far from passion, pain, and guilt,
In a dell 'mid lawny hills,
Which the wild sea-murmur fills,
And soft sunshine, and the sound
Of old forests echoing round,
And the light and smell divine
Of all flowers that breathe and shine :
We may live so happy there,
That the spirits of the air,
Envying us, may even entice
To our healing paradise
The polluting multitude ;
But their rage would be subdued
By that clime divine and calm,

And the winds whose wings rain balm
On the uplifted soul, and leaves
Under which the bright sea heaves:
While each breathless interval
In their whisperings musical
The inspired soul supplies
With its own deep melodies,
And the love which heals all strife
Circling, like the breath of life,
All things in that sweet abode
With its own mild brotherhood:
They, not it would change; and soon
Every sprite beneath the moon
Would repent its envy vain,
And the earth grow young again.

HYMN

TO

INTELLECTUAL BEAUTY.

THE awful shadow of some unseen Power
   Floats tho' unseen among us ; visiting
   This various world with as inconstant wing
As summer winds that creep from flower to
      flower ;
Like moonbeams that behind some piny moun-
     tain shower,
   It visits with inconstant glance
   Each human heart and countenance ;
Like hues and harmonies of evening,
    Like clouds in starlight widely spread,
    Like memory of music fled,
    Like aught that for its grace may be
Dear, and yet dearer for its mystery.

Spirit of BEAUTY, that dost consecrate
　　With thine own hues all thou dost shine upon
　　Of human thought or form, where art thou
　　　　gone ?
Why dost thou pass away and leave our state,
This dim vast vale of tears, vacant and desolate ?
　　　　Ask why the sunlight not forever
　　　　Weaves rainbows o'er yon mountain river
Why aught should fail and fade that once is
　　　　shewn ;
　　　　Why fear and dream and death and birth
　　　　Cast on the daylight of this earth
　　　　Such gloom, why man has such a scope
For love and hate, despondency and hope ?

No voice from some sublimer world hath ever
　　To sage or poet these responses given :
　　Therefore the names of Demon, Ghost, and
　　　　Heaven,
Remain the records of their vain endeavour :
Frail spells, whose uttered charm might not
　　　　avail to sever,

From all we hear and all we see,
Doubt, chance, and mutability.
Thy light alone, like mist o'er mountains driven,
Or music by the night wind sent
Thro' strings of some still instrument,
Or moonlight on a midnight stream,
Gives grace and truth to life's unquiet dream.

Love, Hope, and Self-esteem, like clouds, depart
And come, for some uncertain moments lent.
Man were immortal, and omnipotent,
Didst thou, unknown and awful as thou art,
Keep with thy glorious train firm state within
his heart.
Thou messenger of sympathies
That wax and wane in lover's eyes ;
Thou, that to human thought are nourishment,
Like darkness to a dying flame !
Depart not as thy shadow came :
Depart not, lest the grave should be,
Like life and fear, a dark reality.

While yet a boy I sought for ghosts, and sped
    Thro' many a listening chamber, cave and ruin,
    And starlight wood, with fearful steps pur-
        suing
Hopes of high talk with the departed dead.
I called on poisonous names with which our
        youth is fed :
      I was not heard: I saw them not:
      When musing deeply on the lot
Of life, at that sweet time when winds are wooing
      All vital things that wake to bring
      News of birds and blossoming,
      Sudden, thy shadow fell on me
I shrieked, and clasped my hands in extacy !

I vowed that I would dedicate my powers
    To thee and thine : have I not kept the vow ?
With beating heart and streaming eyes, even
    now
I call the phantoms of a thousand hours
Each from his voiceless grave: they have in
    visioned bowers

Of studious zeal or loves delight
Outwatched with me the envious night :
They know that never joy illumed my brow,
   Unlinked with hope that thou wouldst free
   This world from its dark slavery,
   That thou O awful LOVELINESS,
Wouldst give whate'er these words cannot ex-
   press.

The day becomes more solemn and serene
   When noon is past: there is a harmony
   In autumn, and a lustre in its sky,
Which thro' the summer is not heard or seen,
As if it could not be, as if it had not been !
   Thus let thy power, which like the truth
   Of nature on my passive youth
Descended, to my onward life supply
   Its calm, to one who worships thee,
   And every form containing thee,
   Whom, SPIRIT fair, thy spells did bind
To fear himself, and love all human kind.

SONNET.

OZYMANDIAS.

I MET a traveller from an antique land
Who said : Two vast and trunkless legs of stone
Stand in the desart.   Near them, on the sand,
Half sunk, a shattered visage lies, whose frown,
And wrinkled lip, and sneer of cold command,
Tell that its sculptor well those passions read
Which yet survive, stamped on these lifeless
      things,
The hand that mocked them and the heart that
      fed :
And on the pedestal these words appear :
" My name is Ozymandias, king of kings :
Look on my works, ye Mighty, and despair ! "
Nothing beside remains.   Round the decay
Of that colossal wreck, boundless and bare
The lone and level sands stretch far away.

FINIS.

www.ingramcontent.com/pod-product-compliance
Lightning Source LLC
Chambersburg PA
CBHW032101010726
47493CB00008B/2488